# ONE
## LITTLE
### MOUSE

# ONE
# LITTLE
# MOUSE

by Dori Chaconas

illustrated by LeUyen Pham

VIKING

To Michaela, my own—
with all my love
—D. C.

To Shino Sunshine,
with love from
Uyen-O

VIKING
Published by the Penguin Group
Penguin Putnam Books for Young Readers, 345 Hudson Street,
New York, New York 10014, U.S.A.
Penguin Books Ltd, 80 Strand, London WC2R 0RL, England
Penguin Books Australia Ltd, Ringwood, Victoria, Australia
Penguin Books Canada Ltd, 10 Alcorn Avenue, Toronto, Ontario, Canada M4V 3B2
Penguin Books (N.Z.) Ltd, 182-190 Wairau Road, Auckland 10, New Zealand

Penguin Books Ltd, Registered Offices: Harmondsworth, Middlesex, England

First published in 2002 by Viking, a division of Penguin Putnam Books for Young Readers.

10 9 8 7 6 5 4 3 2 1

LIBRARY OF CONGRESS CATALOGING-IN-PUBLICATION DATA
Chaconas, Dori, date
One little mouse / by Dori Chaconas ; illustrated by LeUyen Pham.
    p.   cm.
Summary: Woodland animals, from two moles to ten opossums, offer to
share their homes with a little mouse who is dissatisfied with his own.
 ISBN 0-670-88947-4
[1. Forest animals—Fiction. 2. Animals—Habitations—Fiction.
3. Counting. 4. Stories in rhyme.] I. Pham, LeUyen, ill. II. Title.
PZ8.3.C345 Op 2002      [E]—dc21      2001006109

Printed in  Hong Kong
Set in Worcester-Round, Packard
Book design by Teresa Kietlinski

The artwork for this book was done in watercolor and
gouache on Arches Cold Press paper.

One little mouse took a look at his house
Deep in the woodland ground.
"This nest is too small! Not roomy at all!
There must be a new one around."

Two blackish moles peeked out of their holes
And called to the mouse passing by,
"We have a fine nest in which you can rest."
So little Mouse thought he would try.

But their diet was wormish,
And that made Mouse squirmish.
He very soon said, "Good-bye."

Three meadow frogs were leaping from logs.
"You'll like sleeping here," they said.
Mouse thanked them politely, but curling up tightly
He found it too cold for a bed.

With a wheeze and a sneeze,
He was sure he would freeze.
"This never will do!" he said.

Four bobwhite quail ran up from the vale.
"If you're looking for someplace to rest,
We have a nice hollow, and if you will follow,
We think we have room for a guest."

But Mouse found it bumpy
And clumpy and lumpy,
Just too many eggs in the nest!

Five greeny snakes from meadows and lakes
Hissed, "Come home with us if you dare!"
"No, thank you," Mouse cried,
And hurried to hide.
Snakes gave him a terrible scare!

Six baby cottontails hopped along hilly trails.
"Come, little Mouse, share our bed."
"Oh thank you," said Mouse. "I'm in need of a house."
And he happily laid down his head.

But the cottontails bunched up
And crunched up and hunched up.
"And soon I'll be scrunched up!" Mouse said.

Seven gray squirrels
Ran in circles and swirls,
Then carried Mouse up to their nest.
"You may stay here with us
If you don't make a fuss."
And Mouse said, "I will do my best."

But the nut nest was clicky
And clacky and cracky.
He left without one bit of rest.

Eight chickadees flew in with the breeze.
"We have a fine place in the willow."
But Mouse said, "Dear me! I can't sleep in a tree!
Imagine a branch for a pillow!"

Nine porcupine waddled by in a line.
They called to the mouse, "Good day!
We have a nice den, right here in the glen."
"Thank you," Mouse answered. "I'll stay."

But their sharp quills were sticking
And picking and pricking.
So Mouse quickly went on his way.

Ten small opossums were eating plum blossoms.
"Come on, sleep with us," they were singing.
They knotted his tail, and Mouse let out a wail
To find himself suddenly swinging.

"A terrible tizzy! I'm upside-down dizzy!
A mouse tail is not made for clinging."

Then Mouse turned around to the darkening wood
And scampered along just as fast as he could,
Back to his own little comfortable house
(So tiny and tidy, just right for a mouse),
And when evening shadows crept over the ground
And covered the woodland, here's what was found:

Ten small opossums asleep in the glen.
Nine porcupine nestled up in their den.
Eight chickadees roosting
High in the willows.
Seven gray squirrels using
Soft tails for pillows.

Six baby cottontails snug in their nest.
Five greeny snakes coiled up for a rest.
Four bobwhite quail very still in the vale.
Three meadow frogs sleeping on logs.
Two blackish moles deep in their holes.

And one little mouse,
One tired little mouse,
One content little mouse,
Sound asleep in his house.